The Magic Key

Clutterland Band

Biff was a winner! She had won a trip in a hot air balloon. Now everyone was ready to go. But where was Biff?

At last, Biff and Nadim arrived, weighed down with all Nadim's cameras.

The pilot took one stern look. 'You can't bring all those heavy things into the balloon. It won't float.'

Nadim was grumpy. He wasn't going to leave any of them behind. So Biff got cross. 'You want them all, but you don't need them all,' she said, 'so just pick one.'

The balloon waited.

I wish he would choose, thought Floppy.

The key on Floppy's collar started to glow.

Biff, Nadim, and Floppy were pulled into a spinning vortex of wonderful lights and colours. They were flying round and round, faster and faster …

Biff, Nadim, and Floppy landed. They were on a small, very flat island, moving through the water. On either side sat a team of rowers. In the middle stood Old Mother Clutter and her husband, surrounded by loads of junk.

They beat time on dustbin drums to cheer on the rowers. 'Row Mary Lou, Mary Sue, Mary Jo, Mary Jean, Mary Jane. Row Bobby Ray, Bobby Jay, Bobby Joe, Bobby John, Bobby Jim. Row straight ahead to Binbag Bay or the Great Green Garbage Gobbler will get us.'

Nadim and Biff peered out at the strange sight, and Nadim took some photos. Biff grabbed him, banging her elbow on an old motor stuck in a pile of junk – and there was even more up ahead. A bigger island was coming into sight, piled high with rubbish. They moored at the jetty of Clutterland.

'We got a whole load of clutter to collect today,' yelled Mother Clutter.

She was interrupted by a weird sound, coming from a dustbin. Father Clutter peered in – it was Floppy squashed inside and howling.

'It's a singing dog!' said Father Clutter.

'No he's not!' said Biff.

‘And who might you be?’ said Mother Clutter suspiciously.

‘I’m Biff,’ said Biff.

‘Well, Mary Biff,’ said Mother Clutter, ‘the Marys and the Bobbys have got to get a-cluttering before the Great Green Garbage Gobbler eats our junk. There’s nothing he’d like more than to get his gobbling jaws on it. And we aren’t going to let him!’

Meanwhile, Mary Jo had spotted an old piano. The Bobbys carried it proudly on to Flatland, put it down, and *SPLASH!*

The Marys and the Bobbys cheered and jumped into their rowing places.

The water covered their ankles and the island began to sink. Biff looked at Nadim, worried.

'You've got to take the piano back!' Biff pleaded.

'Piffle, tosh, and fiddle-dee-dee,' said Mother Clutter and bounced across the junk. Everyone was trying to stay out of the water.

Meanwhile, Father Clutter was lifting Floppy on top of the soggy piano. 'Sing to me, dog,' he said.

Floppy looked down at the rapidly sinking piano. It'll have to be a very short song, he thought.

What were the children to do? Nadim knew. 'We have to get this island close to the Great Green Garbage Gobbler!'

He scrambled over the clutter and found the old motor which he and Biff fitted to the end of the island.

Meanwhile, the piano was now a little island by itself. Father Clutter started to play – and sank waist deep into the water. He and Floppy were stuck – trapped on top of the piano.

'Help!' he yelled. But none of the Bobbys or Marys could swim.

There was a lurch, and a strange noise.

'Hey, what's going on?' shouted Mother Clutter.

The island swung round and started moving back in the opposite direction …

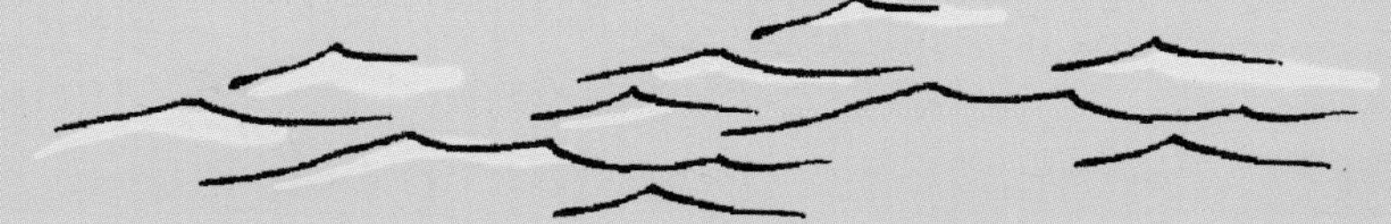

… straight towards the jaws of the Great Green Garbage Gobbler.

'Stop the engine,' yelled Mother Clutter. 'He'll gobble up everything we have!'

Biff faced Mother Clutter. 'Do you really need these ironing boards?' Mother Clutter didn't even do ironing.

The Gobbler was coming nearer and nearer. The Great Green jaws opened. 'Grrrrr!' he roared.

Far away, Father Clutter could be heard, calling for help. He and Floppy were now up to their necks in water.

'That's the idea,' said Nadim. 'If you don't feed him some junk, we'll all drown.'

'Oh, all right then,' scowled Mother Clutter. She picked up an ironing board, rushed down the island and hurled it at the monster. The Gobbler gulped it down.

'Go on then, Clutterband,' called Old Mother Clutter. 'Feed the Gobbler!'

'Yeehaw!' cried the Marys and Bobbys, as all kinds of junk flew through the air into the waiting Gobbler's jaws.

Finally, the Gobbler gave a huge hiccup and was finished.

Later, everyone stood round Mother Clutter on a clean green island.

'We have to thank you for saving us from sinking,' she said to Nadim, and handed him a camera which she'd saved from the clutter. 'But I miss my old clutter heap and that's a fact.'

But Nadim had a present for her – one of the photographs he had taken when they first landed on Flatland, looking just the way it had always looked. Mother Clutter was delighted.

And there was just time for Father Clutter and Floppy to give everyone a sing-song at the piano.

'Yeehaw!' the Clutterband cried. Floppy looked pleased.

'The key's glowing,' said Nadim.

We're going, thought Floppy.

Back at the balloon, Nadim cheerfully unloaded all his cameras and left Floppy to guard them.

Who do you think I am, thought Floppy. The Great Green Camera Gobbler?

And now they were off. The balloon rose slowly into the air.

'Yeehaw!' cried Gran.

Biff and Nadim stared at each other!

As they drifted up, Nadim got out his camera and leaned over the side of the basket.

'Smile, Bobby Floppy,' he called and took a photo.

At least I don't have to sing, thought Floppy.

OXFORD
UNIVERSITY PRESS

Great Clarendon Street, Oxford OX2 6DP

Oxford University Press is a department of the University of Oxford.
It furthers the University's objective of excellence in research, scholarship,
and education by publishing worldwide in

Oxford New York

Athens Auckland Bankok Bogotá Buenos Aires
Cape Town Chennai Dar es Salaam Delhi Florence Hong Kong Istanbul
Kolkata Karachi Kuala Lumpur Madrid Melbourne Mexico City Mumbai
Nairobi Paris São Paulo Singapore Taipei Tokyo Toronto Warsaw

with associated companies in Berlin Ibadan

Based on characters in the Oxford Reading Tree Series written by Roderick Hunt and illustrated by Alex Brychta and published by Oxford University Press
Text by Diane Redmond. Illustrations by Specs Art

First published 2000

British Library Cataloguing in Publication Data available
ISBN 0-19-272432-0
3 5 7 9 10 8 6 4 2